One for All

Evelyn Coleman

Illustrated by Nancy Pelham Foulke

Rigby

Contents

1

Tessa Reese, Room Monitor

"Tessa Reese, what is the capital of Georgia?" Mrs. Varner asked.

"Atlanta," Tessa replied.

"Yes, that's correct, Tessa. Phyllis, what is the capital of . . ."

Tessa heard a static interruption coming over the loudspeaker. "Mrs. Varner, would you please come to the office?"

"Tessa, I believe it's your turn to be the room monitor," Mrs. Varner said. "Everyone, please put your heads on your desks and be quiet. When I walk back in this room I expect to see you acting like fourth graders."

Tessa immediately laid her head on her

folded arms on the desk. She listened to Mrs. Varner's clicking steps moving toward the door. She heard the door opening and closing shut. And then it was silent. She didn't think fourth graders should have to put their heads on their desks. Second graders, maybe, but fourth graders? No way.

Gradually, voices and the sound of scuffling feet filled the room. The noise grew louder and louder and louder until Tessa said, "You all better sit down and be quiet. You heard what Mrs. Varner said."

Her plea changed nothing. In fact, Tessa was sure everyone got even louder. She wished her classmates would sit down and be quiet. But she heard even more talking. Suddenly, laughing and giggling erupted as Tessa felt the whoosh of something fly near her head. Tessa shouted, "And don't throw anything. You're going to get us all in trouble."

Bailey, Tessa's best friend, sat directly behind Tessa. And even she was talking loudly to Phyllis, Tessa's other best friend. Tessa turned around and said, "Please, Bailey and Phyllis, you're both going to get in trouble. Stop talking." It was a waste of air.

Tessa laid her head back onto her folded arms and wished Mrs. Varner would hurry back. Actually, she wished that her classmates would all just do what they were told. Even Bailey and Phyllis didn't care that their own best friend had asked them to be quiet. It will serve them right if they get in trouble, Tessa thought.

Tessa flinched when she heard the door creaking open. All the other kids were making too much noise to notice.

"OK, that's it," Mrs. Varner said. "Tessa," she continued in her "I'm not playing around" voice, "did you ask the class to be quiet and sit down?"

Tessa could feel Mrs. Varner standing next to her, tapping lightly on the back of her chair. Tessa didn't sit up. She wished at this moment that Mrs. Varner had chosen someone else to be room monitor.

"Tessa, did you hear my question?" Mrs. Varner asked again.

Mrs. Varner didn't treat Tessa any differently because Tessa was blind. Some of Tessa's teachers seemed to cut her a little slack, but not Mrs. Varner. Tessa liked that. But right now Tessa wished for a bit of compassion.

"Yes, I did," Tessa said with little enthusiasm. But Tessa knew that she gave the right answer. If she'd told a lie, her mother would know it. Somehow her mother knew everything. Tessa had often wondered if her mother didn't have some well-placed spies in the school. Plus, it always bothered Tessa if she didn't tell the truth.

Tessa cringed when she heard Mrs. Varner announce, "You all know you have no excuse for the way you acted. So, no recess tomorrow."

Moans and groans escaped from the kids' mouths, almost as loud as their laughing and giggling had been.

"Tessa," Mrs. Varner said, "since you were the room monitor and you *tried* to do your job well, I'm going to let you go out at recess. You, Sefu, and Dini were the only people I saw sitting quietly. So all three of you will go out for recess. Now everyone, let's get ready to go home."

Sefu and Dini were twin girls who were

new to the school. They came from Ethiopia and always got the highest grades on tests. Bailey and Phyllis said the twins were always trying to show up everyone when it came to answering the teacher. So far, they hadn't made too many friends at school.

Tessa's thoughts shifted to tomorrow's recess. Tessa had planned on practicing her running at recess with Bailey and Phyllis. Tessa had joined the track team this year and wanted to get in as much practice as she could in the two weeks before the track meet. And now Bailey and Phyllis had to stay in for recess. Why hadn't they listened to Mrs. Varner?

2

Track Practice

Tessa stuffed her things inside her backpack. She grabbed her white cane and said, "Phyllis, Bailey, I'll meet you at your lockers. You're helping me at track today, right?"

"Right," the girls replied. "We'll be there in a minute."

Tessa walked into the hall, allowing her white cane to sweep back and forth in front of her on the way to her locker. At her locker, Tessa spun the tumbler of her special lock. She listened carefully for the lock's clicks and lined up her secret combination by feeling the tabs.

Tessa walked down the hall toward Bailey

and Phyllis' lockers. She gently tapped the lockers on her left, then the water fountain, three doorways, and some more lockers. The chatter of other kids surrounded Tessa as she counted her steps.

Suddenly a boy shouted to Tessa, "Watch out with that cane, girl."

Tessa hated that. She had to sweep the cane back and forth to keep from walking or stumbling into an object. And it was only reasonable that sometimes the cane bumped into a person's foot. That's why it was important to tap close to the floor so that no one would be hit in the shins or the knees. But sometimes kids got mad if the cane accidentally touched their feet.

When Tessa counted her steps to lockers 202 and 203, she knew she was standing right in front of her two best friends' lockers. "Bailey, Phyllis, you there?" Tessa called.

"Yes, we're here," Phyllis said.

"Are you ready to go to track practice with me?" Tessa asked.

"Well, I guess we need some exercise since *some* of us aren't going out to recess tomorrow," Bailey said.

"Don't blame me. I warned you not to talk in class, remember?" Tessa protested.

"All right, Miss Room Monitor," Bailey said. "Hey, do you know if Kathy is practicing today?"

Tessa shrugged. "Kathy who? And why do you need to know?"

"I'll tell you later," Bailey said. "I can't stay long, though."

Tessa said, "That's OK. Coach Carolyn just wants to show you how to be a guide runner. Then we can go home."

After the girls changed into shorts and T-shirts, Tessa walked with Bailey and Phyllis down to the field, which was in back of the school. The brick school building was shaped like the letter L. A teacher always stood at the long end of the L watching the field, just to make sure the kids were behaving themselves. Today the science teacher, Miss Robinson, was on duty.

As they passed Miss Robinson, Bailey asked, "Miss Robinson, did Kathy Walker come past yet?"

Kathy Walker was in sixth grade and was the president of the entire student body.

"Bailey, why do you keep asking about Kathy?" Tessa asked.

Phyllis answered, "Because she'll be choosing two fourth-grade students to get Good Citizenship Awards and go to the awards ceremony that the school district is having. You didn't know that?"

"No, I didn't," Tessa replied.

Tessa used her cane to navigate her way as she walked across the track with Bailey and Phyllis. The black, soft surface of the track made Tessa feel like little springs were inside her shoes. She loved running on this track. It was much better than the old one. That one had tiny rocks that really hurt whenever she fell.

The track was ringed with a large oval of short-cut grass. Tessa found the wire fence that surrounded the grass and the track, and propped her cane against it. Tessa didn't need it now, and she didn't want anyone to stumble over it.

Tessa plopped down on the grass and pulled her shoes out of her backpack. They were brand new running shoes. Tessa put them on. The new shoes felt stiff and tight and still needed to be broken in.

Tessa heard the thud of shoes approaching from her left.

"Hi, Tessa. It's me, Coach Carolyn."

"Hello, Coach," Tessa said. Coach Carolyn understood that people who were blind didn't have magic hearing and couldn't identify everyone's footsteps. Coach Carolyn knew it was important to identify herself when she walked up to a blind person, and also to let them know when she was leaving.

Coach Carolyn said, "I'm glad you're here, Tessa. Are these girls your guide runners?"

"Yes, they are," Tessa said. "Coach Carolyn, I'd like you to meet my friends, Bailey and Phyllis. They're not experienced guide runners, but they'd like to learn."

Coach Carolyn said, "Nice to meet you girls. Tessa asked me to let you two try out. I'll show you both everything a guide runner does, but you'll run with Tessa only one at a time. If Tessa has a good guide runner to help her, she might be able to run against the other school's team in the next big meet."

"I will?" Tessa cried. Last year, the coach wouldn't allow her on the team. He said he felt it would be too dangerous for Tessa to run. But this year Coach Carolyn had welcomed Tessa to the team. Coach Carolyn had experience with other people who were blind. Before coming to this school, she was the gym teacher and track coach at a school for the blind in Connecticut.

It was important to Tessa to run well. She would prove that she could run on a regular team. All Tessa needed was a good guide runner to help her stay on the track and she was set. It was what Tessa had dreamed of— to run against sighted kids on a regular track team.

"OK, girls, let's warm up," Coach Carolyn said.

Bailey and Phyllis followed the coach's lead while Tessa listened carefully to her directions. Tessa stretched her legs out in front of her and rotated her ankles. She stood back up and flexed the muscles in the back of her legs. Tessa ran in place for a minute or two. Then it was time to begin.

"Are you ready, Bailey?" Coach Carolyn asked. "You can go first."

"Sure," Bailey said. "What do I do?"

Tessa felt a little nervous. The problem was that neither Bailey nor Phyllis knew much about track. Even though they'd offered to help, Tessa knew that neither of them would have joined the team if Tessa hadn't asked.

"What I want you to do is to run beside Tessa on the track. You're going to hold the tether," the coach explained.

Bailey looked at the tether and asked, "You mean this shoestring thing?"

"Yes, that's a tether," Coach Carolyn continued. "You hold one end and Tessa holds the other end. You're going to run next to her,

holding your end of the tether. You've got to run straight and not sway toward the edge of the track. And you've got to remember to keep the tether pulled tightly between you and Tessa. That helps to keep Tessa in her lane. When you stop, that's a signal for Tessa to stop. You got it?"

"Got it," Bailey said.

"Oh, one more thing," the coach said. "Watch out for the sixth graders who are already out there on the track."

Tessa grabbed her end of the tether and held the other end for Bailey to take. Tessa could feel the other end still dangling.

"Bailey, you've got to take the other end in your hand, please," Coach Carolyn said, a little less patiently.

"Oh yeah. Sorry," Bailey said, taking her end of the tether. "I was trying to untangle my new bracelets."

Phyllis said, "Let me see them. Wow. They're pretty."

"Bailey, Phyllis, please. Let's pay attention. This is important," said the coach.

Tessa knelt into position, flexing her ankle back and forth.

"Phyllis, you can help out, too," Tessa said. "Say: 'Runners take your marks. Get set. Go.'"

"Can't I just say, 'Run'? It sounds silly to say 'runners.' There are only two of you. Do I have to say that?" Phyllis asked.

Tessa frowned. Was the whole practice going to be this way? "OK, Phyllis. Just say: 'Ready. Set. Go.'"

Phyllis said, "All right. Ready. Set. Go."

"Let's go," Coach Carolyn said, and the girls snapped to attention. "Are you ready, Bailey? You're running in the lane on Tessa's right. You've got to run at least as fast as she does. And the guide runner cannot cross the finish line before Tessa. If she did, Tessa would be disqualified in a real race. Now, please pull the tether a little tighter," the coach said. "You're going to run two laps around the track."

Tessa knelt back into her position. Her left leg felt heavy. That happened sometimes because she favored her cane on that side.

"Ready. Set. Go," Phyllis shouted.

Tessa felt the tug on the string. She ran fast and sure of herself because Bailey ran alongside her, holding the other end of the tether. Tessa could feel the tension in the tether. Great. If Bailey allowed too much slack between the two of them, Tessa wouldn't know that Bailey was there, and worse, Tessa might drift into another lane.

Tessa sped forward, her legs loosening up. She thought she heard Coach Carolyn shouting something from the starting line. Suddenly Tessa could no longer feel the taut string. She stumbled and then stopped, just as somebody ran into her. She stretched out her arms to break her fall. The track smacked her face, making it sting like an attack from a hoard of angry bees.

Tessa heard the other runner on the track saying, "I'm sorry. I didn't mean to make you fall. I didn't know you were going to stop."

Tessa felt a hand on her elbow, smelled a lilac scent, and heard a new voice.

"Here," the voice said, "let me help you up."

Bailey whispered, "What did you stop for, Tessa? I just turned around to wave to Phyllis to let her know that Kathy was on the track."

Tessa sighed loudly. "You let the tether go. I had to stop. Coach Carolyn says I'm supposed to stop if my guide runner stops."

"Oh, right," Bailey said, sounding irritated. Then she turned to Kathy. "Tessa didn't mean to mess up your practice, Kathy. Did you Tessa?"

Tessa couldn't believe Bailey. What was she talking about? This was Tessa's practice, too.

Kathy said, "It's OK. I'm cool. Tessa, is it? If you're OK, then I'm going to take off."

Tessa replied, "I'm fine. Thanks."

Tessa pushed herself up with the palms of her hands, which were still stinging from the fall. She brushed off her clothes. Her knee burned. Tessa knew she'd broken the skin. "Am I bleeding?" she asked.

"Hey, where is Kathy going?" Phyllis shouted as she ran to Tessa and Bailey. "That was my chance to meet her."

Phyllis and Bailey seemed more interested in Kathy than in learning to be good guide runners. Tessa wished she didn't feel so angry inside. Her stomach felt like a bouncing ball. She didn't like the feeling she was getting. She remembered that Kathy was the one who would choose the two fourth graders who would get Good Citizenship Awards. Thinking about that *and* her friends' behavior on the track made her feel uneasy.

"Hey, we only get to see her at lunchtime, and since she's in the sixth grade, she sits at a sixth-grade table. If she doesn't know who we are, how can she choose us to get the Good Citizenship Awards?" Phyllis said.

"You ruined it," Bailey said to Tessa. "You didn't have to say you were all right. She probably would have stayed and talked to us. She chooses in a month and anybody who gets picked is automatically cool."

"Yeah," Phyllis agreed.

Tessa's chest tightened.

Coach Carolyn approached the girls and announced, "Sorry, girls. I'm going to have to cut practice short today. Let's try again after school tomorrow."

Tessa's friends walked her toward the grass that led to the wire fence. She had left her cane leaning near the fence's gate, so she used her "bumpers" to feel her way to the entrance. She called her hands "bumpers" when she used them like the cane to bump into objects to find her way. As Tessa checked along the fence, she smelled the sweetness of the honeysuckle as she felt the vine twisting and turning on the wire fence. Tessa used her sense of smell as well as touch to tell her where she was.

As Tessa reached the gate and picked up her cane, she could hear Coach Carolyn saying something to Bailey and Phyllis. She couldn't make out the words, but the coach's voice sounded serious.

Tessa waited for their conversation to end and then called out, "Bailey, Phyllis, are you ready to go home now?"

As Tessa tapped her way toward home with Bailey and Phyllis, she wondered what Coach Carolyn had said to her friends. For some reason, she was afraid to ask. Tessa decided to try and shake her worries, and told herself that tomorrow's practice would be better.

3

Justin's Idea

When Tessa got home, she went to her room, changed her clothes, and began her homework. She heard Justin, her seven-year-old brother, coming in from his after-school program, slamming doors as usual. A minivan from the program dropped him off at the door each day. Tessa was glad she didn't have to go to the after-school program anymore. It was a sign that she was growing up.

"Tessa, it's time for dinner," her mom called. Tessa's mom worked at a bank as a teller. She was also going to school to get a master's degree in business.

At dinner, Tessa explained to her mom what had happened at school. When she finished, her mom said, "You did the right thing as room monitor, honey. I'm so proud of you. Your dad will be, too."

Tessa's dad was a fireman. Being a fireman meant he worked really weird hours, like four days off and three days on. Sometimes Tessa wished he were home more. Her mom was right, though. He would be very proud that she told the truth.

Tessa's pleasure at her mother's praise was mixed with her uneasy feelings about track practice. Would Bailey and Phyllis work out as guide runners?

Tessa's mom interrupted her thoughts. "Is something else bothering you?" she asked.

Tessa described the shortened track practice and her concern over the coach's private conversation with her friends.

"Don't worry about Bailey and Phyllis. Give them a chance. It was only their first try at being guide runners. But if you really think your friends may not be the best guides, maybe you can find someone else to help you practice," Tessa's mom suggested.

"Mom, you don't understand. Phyllis and Bailey are my best friends. We do everything together. We're a team." Tessa argued.

"OK, then. I don't know what to tell you. My suggestion is to think about it while you wash and dry the dishes."

"But Mom, it's not my turn to do the dishes."

"Really? Do you want to wear your favorite shirt tomorrow?"

"Yes, Mom."

"Then I suggest you take my turn at the dishes. Otherwise, I won't have time to iron your shirt and still do my homework."

"It's not fair. And I know . . . 'Sometimes life isn't fair,'" Tessa said, rising from the table to clear the dishes. She didn't like doing dishes by hand, but the dishwasher was broken. The plumber hadn't fixed it yet. It seemed that since her mother had gone back to school, there was always just one more chore added to Tessa's list.

Tessa thought about the idea of having someone else help her with track practice. But Bailey and Phyllis were her best friends. And they said they wanted to help her. The truth was, though, Bailey and Phyllis had changed in some ways. Since they all had turned ten, things seemed different. Now Bailey spent more time talking about things like boys and clothes and things that never mattered before. But it wasn't even that she talked about those things so much as that it was the boys *she* liked, *her* clothes, what *she* wanted to do, where *she* wanted to go, and just about anything else, as long as it had to do with *her*. It was almost like no one else existed. Everything centered around *her*. And Phyllis just seemed to follow Bailey. Whatever Bailey said, Phyllis said, too. Tessa wished things were back the way they were—when it was "one for all and all for one." That was Tessa's line. It was from *The Three Musketeers,* one of Tessa's favorite stories.

Tessa finished her work in the kitchen and then trudged to her room. She couldn't believe the phone hadn't rung. Normally Bailey or Phyllis called Tessa right after dinner. But neither of them called her tonight. Tessa pulled out her stylus—which was like a big pushpin—and her Braille journal, and began writing in it.

One of the good things about her

blindness was that she'd learned Braille. She could write anything and her mom would never figure out what it said. Tessa was the only one in the family with a "secret code."

Tessa moved both her left and right hands along the lines, using her index fingers to

read her journal. She always reread what she'd written in her journal the day before. Tessa was a very fast reader. She could already read 125 words per minute, which was the average for adults.

After reading, Tessa picked up her stylus and began describing her day by punching holes into the paper to form letters and words. She wrote about her disastrous experience as room monitor and how Bailey and Phyllis might not work out as guide runners.

Tessa was so involved in her writing that she practically jumped out of her seat when Justin burst through the door, yelling her name.

"I'm telling Mom you didn't knock," Tessa said angrily. "Do I ever come in your room without knocking?"

Justin ignored her and said, "Mom told me you're worried about your guide runners. Well, I've got some good news for you."

"What?" she asked as she punched in two more words. Her mind was focused on what she wanted to write.

"Your troubles are over. I'll be your guide

runner," Justin said. "Then I won't have to go to the after-school program and I can walk home with you. It'll be great."

Tessa stopped and turned toward her brother. "Thanks, Justin, it's nice of you to offer, but you're not big enough yet," Tessa said, smiling at the thought of a first-grade guide runner.

Justin clearly did not like her answer. But he didn't give up easily when he thought he could solve a problem.

"OK, I've got another idea."

"Really? And what brainy idea is it this time?" Tessa teased.

"My buddy, Mohammed, says his twin sisters Dini and Sefu like to run," Justin continued.

"Mohammed?" Tessa asked.

"Mohammed. You know, my friend who comes over to play with me sometimes. Remember him? His sisters could, you know, be your guides in track practice. They're in your class."

Tessa didn't know that Justin knew the twins' brother. Even though Mohammed was Justin's friend, she wouldn't feel comfortable asking the twins to help. She wasn't very friendly with them. Why would they want to help her? Besides, she had to give Bailey and Phyllis a chance. They were her best friends. How could Tessa split up The Three Musketeers?

4

A Problem

The next day, out of loyalty to her friends, Tessa volunteered to stay in for recess with the rest of the class.

Mrs. Varner eyed Tessa suspiciously. "Tessa, I don't think that's a good idea. You go on outside with Dini and Sefu."

Tessa felt as if all the air left her body. She grabbed her history book from under the desk and found her way outside.

Once she was outside, Tessa settled on a bench. She heard someone approaching. Dini and Sefu stopped short of the bench and leaned up against the schoolyard fence.

As Tessa's fingers swept across the pages, she could hear the twins chatting nearby. She couldn't concentrate on her reading because thoughts were racing through her head about track practice and running on the team. After all, she only had a few weeks before the big meet with Palmer Elementary.

Tessa remembered what Justin had said about the twins. They liked to run. Maybe I should say something to them, Tessa thought. But just then the bell rang. Tessa gathered her cane and her history book and

started in. As Tessa walked back into the classroom, the twins caught up to her.

"We hear you are on the track team," Dini said. "That's great. We both like to run, too."

"Yes," agreed Sefu. "We are hoping to get on the team next year."

"Oh, that sounds great," Tessa said, but she wasn't sure what else to say to the girls. She felt a little badly for them. It was hard to be the new kids at school, and she thought maybe they were having a hard time making friends.

After school, Tessa and her friends met for track practice with Coach Carolyn.

"Hello, ladies," Coach Carolyn said. "Are we ready to try again?"

The coach handed the tether to Bailey. "Do you remember what to do?"

"I think so," Bailey replied, a little hesitantly.

"Remember to keep the tether taut and run at Tessa's pace," the coach instructed.

Bailey got into the lane alongside Tessa at the starting line.

"All right, Phyllis, say 'Ready. Set. Go,'" Coach Carolyn said.

"Ready. Set. Go," shouted Phyllis obediently.

Tessa took off at full speed, and at first, felt secure as Bailey kept the tether in just the right position. Then Tessa felt her tether arm being pulled behind her. Bailey was lagging behind. Tessa was a much faster runner, and Bailey was slowing her down.

After they ran the two laps, Tessa and Bailey returned to the starting line, where the coach and Phyllis stood waiting.

"Way off your time, Tessa," Coach Carolyn said. Tessa could hear the concern in her voice. "You're up, Phyllis. Try to remember everything I told Bailey yesterday."

Phyllis took up the tether and ran the next couple of laps with Tessa.

"Better," Coach Carolyn said.

Practice continued with four more laps. Bailey and Phyllis took turns as guide runner. The results were the same as the first two sets of laps—Phyllis kept up a good pace with Tessa, but Bailey was way too slow.

After Coach Carolyn announced the end of practice for the day, she pulled Bailey and Tessa aside as Phyllis changed into her street shoes.

"I'm sorry to say this, Bailey, but it's just not working out. It was great of you to volunteer to help Tessa, but you're slowing her down. She'll never be able to keep up with the team. I'm sorry."

Bailey stormed back to Phyllis, who was waiting at the fence. "The coach says I can't be a guide runner," Bailey said, frowning. "Who cares, anyway?" she added, but in Tessa's opinion, not too convincingly.

"Well, if *you* can't be a guide runner, then I don't want to be one, either," said Phyllis.

"Phyllis, Bailey, you can't do that! What am I going to do?" asked Tessa.

The girls didn't respond as they gathered up their things and headed home in silence. This is a disaster, thought Tessa. There was no doubt in Tessa's mind that things couldn't get any worse.

5

A Solution

At dinner that night, Tessa ate in silence as she thought of a solution to her problem. She wanted to keep Bailey and Phyllis as guide runners more than anything, but because of Coach Carolyn's decision to drop Bailey, and since Phyllis always followed what Bailey did, it didn't look like that would happen. She had to find a good guide runner to replace her friends. Later that evening, she asked Justin to help her carry out her plan.

"Justin, I lost Phyllis and Bailey as my guide runners. But I have an idea. I need you to help me make a sign. If you help, you get to come to my class after school. Plus, you can be my manager."

Justin looked suspicious. "Manager of what? What kind of sign?"

Tessa filled Justin in on all the details of her plan. They worked together on the wording of Tessa's sign. Then Justin read the finished sign to her. It was perfect.

WANTED
Guide Runner
Interview Today!
After School in Mrs. Varner's room
— - o — o — o — o —
Tessa Reese will interview any 4th grader for a job as a guide runner. Prefer someone who likes track and can run fast. Must be able to practice after school 2 days a week.

The next morning, as soon as Tessa arrived at school, she approached Mrs. Varner and asked, "May I put up a sign on the announcement board?" Any student could put a sign on Mrs. Varner's board, as long as they had her approval. Sometimes kids sold used comics, trading cards, or stuff they just didn't want anymore.

"Let me read it, Tessa," Mrs. Varner said. "I'll let you know by lunchtime if you can post it." When Mrs. Varner gave Tessa the OK, she helped Tessa post the sign. Later that day, Tessa's hopes grew as kids asked her questions.

"How much are you paying?" a boy asked.

She was paying her entire allowance—$5.00 for two one-hour practices a week.

"What do you have to do, exactly?" another classmate wondered.

"A guide runner runs alongside me holding a string between us so I won't run off the track," Tessa answered.

When class was over, Mrs. Varner even let Tessa sit at her desk to do the interviews. Mrs. Varner sat at a desk in the back of the room, checking papers.

Justin showed up just in time. He'd gotten special permission to come to Tessa's room.

"Hey, Sis. You ready? Got your interview questions ready to ask?" Justin asked.

"Yes. Will you ask everyone to get in line so we can start?"

"Line?" Justin asked.

"Yes, line. We have to be orderly," Tessa said. "I want to do this right."

Justin shouted, "Everyone please line up."

Tessa didn't hear very much commotion. She panicked. Maybe there wasn't anyone to line up. She pulled Justin close to her. "There *is* someone here, right?"

"Yep," he said, chuckling.

His laugh made Tessa nervous. She said, "All right, would the first person take a seat?"

Tessa heard the rustle of the person's clothes as they sat down. She smelled the faint odor of a flowery shampoo. She figured it was a girl.

"Please tell me your name," Tessa asked, "and why you want this job."

"This is Dini. Remember me? We talked at recess the other day. I like running track and I'd like to help you because I've seen you run and I think you could be a great runner."

Tessa thought that was a good answer. She said, "Thanks, Dini. I'll let you know after I talk to everyone else. Next." She heard the chair scraping as Dini got up and another person sat down.

"What's your name?" Tessa asked. "And why do you want this job?"

"This is Dini's sister, Sefu. I guess I want to help because you need the help. I'd want someone to help me."

Tessa, not sure what to ask next, replied, "Thank you, Sefu. I'll let you know. Next."

Justin touched her shoulder and whispered, "That's it."

Tessa's head shot up. "What? That was it? Only two people showed?" Tessa straightened her shoulders and said to Justin, "Would you ask Dini and Sefu to come back for a minute?"

Tessa heard another chair being pulled up to Mrs. Varner's desk and the twins settling into them. "Uh, I really appreciate you two applying for the job. I need someone who can help me next year, too. Will both of you be on the team next year?"

Dini said, "Yes, but that's no problem. Coach Carolyn said we could still help you next year."

"Oh, I see," Tessa said, wondering what question she could ask next. Tessa squeezed her cane's handle. Then a thought came to her. Tessa squared her shoulders and stated, "I need someone who is comfortable with a visually impaired person."

Again it was Dini who answered. "We're very comfortable with blind people. Our grandmother is blind, but she's like any seeing person. She even takes karate lessons."

Well, this is just too good to be true, Tessa thought. How could she *not* pick them for guide runners?

"OK, you've got the job, if Coach Carolyn approves, of course," Tessa announced, hoping her problems were solved.

6

New Problem, New Plan

Later that afternoon, Tessa did her homework and then went out to the backyard to sit on her swing. Gently swinging back and forth helped her to think. She wondered what Bailey and Phyllis would say about her new guide runners.

Tessa knew her backyard as well as she knew the layout of her house. The garden was full of color—green, pink, white, and red. Even though Tessa didn't know what the colors looked like, she knew the grass and flowers by their smells. She liked the strong fragrance of the flowers, but some of them made her nose twitch. The honeysuckles were her favorites. Two of the pine trees had a fresh scent that Tessa loved, too, but they dropped pinecones onto the garden walk. Sometimes the cones caused Tessa to stumble as she walked along the path.

It was funny, really. Some people thought it was some kind of miracle that Tessa could do things like run track, or learn to write the same letters and words that sighted people did. But her Orientation and Mobility teacher taught her all those things.

Tessa had a special class with Mrs. Carter, her O&M teacher. Tessa left her regular classroom every day to have a session with Mrs. Carter. Mrs. Carter showed her how to use sounds, odors, temperatures, or objects to touch as clues in finding her way around. For example, Tessa knew Bailey always used a strawberry rinse in her hair, while Phyllis smelled like the peppermint gum or candy she always chewed on.

Tessa paid attention to details that others might not notice. She also had to be a little more careful with her stuff than other kids were. She kept her closet and her desk at school organized so she could find things easily. Tessa didn't think she was extraordinary because she was blind—it was just a part of the person she was.

Tessa rocked back and forth on her swing, thinking about how she could show Bailey and Phyllis that they were still her best friends even though she now had new guide runners.

After dinner, Tessa excused herself from the table and headed to her room. She decided to sit down and write to her pen pal Sabrina. It was so much fun exchanging Braille letters with Sabrina. Sabrina was ten years old, too. They had met at summer camp last year and discovered they had a lot in common. For example, they both loved riding their bikes and getting involved in other sports. Thanks to Tessa's suggestion, Sabrina was now playing Beep Baseball in her hometown of Bangor, Maine.

Tessa had explained to Sabrina that Beep Baseball is a game for the visually impaired that is played like regular baseball, but has its own special equipment and rules. The ball and bases make beeping sounds to help the batter and the fielders hit or catch the ball. After a batter hits a ball, he or she only has to run to one base to score a point. A sighted person decides which base should beep, and then the batter runs toward that one.

Tessa thought Sabrina would like the game as much as Tessa did, and it turned out that Sabrina did. Sabrina loved the game and always wrote to Tessa with the latest Beep Baseball news.

Tessa loved playing Beep Baseball with her team, the Claymore Diamonds. The team was made up of kids from all over the county. Tessa loved the way the team worked together. They were a real team. Everyone helped each other out. Those players that had a bit more sight helped those who had no sight at all. It was a great feeling to be on a team where everyone looked out for each other.

Tessa pulled out her stylus and paper and began a letter to Sabrina. She hoped Sabrina might have some advice for her.

In Braille, Tessa wrote:

Dear Sabrina,

I have a little problem, and I hope you can give me some advice. My two best friends were going to be my guide runners for track this year, but it's not working out. Bailey is too slow and the coach won't let her run with me. And Phyllis won't do it if Bailey doesn't. There are two other girls in my class who want to be my guide runners, but I'm afraid that if I let them, then Bailey and Phyllis will be mad at me and won't be my friends anymore. What do you think I should do?

I hope everything's OK with you. Are you still playing Beep Baseball?

Write soon.

Love,
Tessa

Tessa sealed the envelope and used a special guide to keep her writing in the right place when she wrote Sabrina's address on the envelope. She and Sabrina enjoyed putting short, funny Braille messages on the back flaps of the envelope. They wished they could see the mail people trying to figure out what the dots were.

The next day at lunchtime, Tessa told Bailey and Phyllis that her new guide runners were the new kids in school, Dini and Sefu.

"I'd rather have you two as my guide runners," said Tessa.

"Sure," replied Bailey, "but it wasn't *my* idea to quit."

"Yeah," said Phyllis, "it wasn't Bailey's idea."

"So why *did* you pick the twins?" Bailey asked. "No, don't tell me. I know. They're perfect at everything. They always have the right answers in class. They're probably the best runners, too," Bailey said. "Well, go ahead and be friends with them if you want."

So Bailey was jealous of Dini and Sefu. That was what Tessa was afraid of. It didn't make sense to her, but it still hurt.

Tessa met up with her friends at their lockers at the end of the school day, as usual. But as Tessa suspected, Bailey was still angry. Phyllis and Bailey both said they had other plans and couldn't walk Tessa home as usual. Tessa spent the entire evening moping around her house.

Then she had an idea. Tessa's spirits lifted a bit when she decided to put her plan into action the next day. She would show Bailey and Phyllis that no matter what, The Three Musketeers would never split up.

7

Patience, Please

On Friday morning, Tessa hurried to the principal's office. Tessa didn't need anyone to show her the way, like she had when she first came to this school. She was glad of that. Tessa could get to where she needed to go on her own.

When Tessa arrived at the principal's office, Kathy Walker was still making the class announcements over the speaker system. That was part of what the president of the student government got to do. Tessa waited nervously outside the office door. When Tessa heard footsteps close by and smelled the lilac scent, she spoke. "Excuse me, Kathy, would you mind if I talked to you for a minute?"

Kathy said, "Hey, it's you. I ran into you the other day. And I *do* mean ran into you. I'm sorry about that. I hope you're OK. I didn't mean to make you fall."

"I . . . uh . . . no. No, I'm fine. My name's Tessa Reese." Tessa could hear herself tripping over her words.

"Tessa, did you want to tell me something? I've got to get to class," Kathy said.

"Yes. I . . . uh, wanted to say that I know the two perfect fourth graders for the Good Citizenship Awards," Tessa began.

"Really? Who are they?"

Tessa continued. "Phyllis and Bailey. They're terrific. They're my best friends."

"You mean the two girls who were with you the other day?"

"Yes," Tessa said. "I sure hope you pick them. Their names are Bailey Whiteside and Phyllis Cowan. Will you think about it?"

Kathy said, "Well, I saw them helping you at practice that day. They didn't seem very patient."

Tessa stumbled a bit. "Well, OK, they didn't work out as guide runners, but they are really great friends and they do lots of good things, and I know you'd think so, too, if you got to know them."

"Well, I'll keep them in mind. Now I've got to run. See you around, Tessa."

"See you around," Tessa said, encouraged. It sounded like Kathy would give Bailey and Phyllis some consideration.

After school, Dini and Sefu met Tessa and Coach Carolyn at the track for their first practice. Coach Carolyn pulled Tessa aside to speak with her. "Where is your friend Phyllis?"

Tessa explained that Phyllis quit because of Bailey. She couldn't help blurting out her feelings about how Bailey and Phyllis were acting toward her.

"Tessa, I understand. I'm sure Bailey is just as upset as you are right now. You'll work it out," the coach reassured Tessa.

That made Tessa feel a little better.

"OK, let's get started," the coach said.

The twins had to be told how to use the tether. That took a little practice before they got it right. But Dini and Sefu were fast runners. They had to slow down so they wouldn't yank Tessa off her feet. Tessa liked the challenge of pushing herself to run even faster.

As she ran, Coach Carolyn yelled to Tessa from the sidelines. "Stay on the balls of your feet," the coach shouted. "Lean forward, bend your knees. Bring them up and put them down."

The practice went great. Tessa enjoyed working with Dini and Sefu, and she was hopeful that things would work out with Phyllis and Bailey.

Tessa was up in her room after dinner that night, reading the last pages in her book, when her mom called her. Tessa laid the book down and walked out of her room. "Yes, Mom?" she called, hoping her mom was calling her to come eat the banana pudding she had been making.

"You've got company," her mom said.

"I knew Bailey and Phyllis wouldn't stay mad forever," Tessa said, walking into the room with a grin on her face.

But her mom said, "It's not Phyllis or Bailey. It's Mohammed's sisters."

Tessa was speechless.

"Well, what are you waiting for?" Tessa's mom asked. "You've been moping around here for a few days now, wishing for someone to play with. And now you have two new friends waiting to visit with you."

"I don't feel like playing or visiting with *anyone,* Mom," Tessa said. She was completely disappointed that the visitors weren't Bailey and Phyllis.

"What's wrong with you, Tessa?" her mom asked. "Where are your manners?"

"That's all right, Mrs. Reese. We'll come back another time," Tessa heard Sefu say.

"We brought you something," Dini said. "We'll just leave it for you."

Tessa could hear the sadness in Dini's voice. And it made Tessa feel terrible inside, so she forced herself to say, "Thank you, but you didn't have to bring me anything."

Sefu said, "We know. It was Dini's idea, not mine."

"Well, still, thank you," Tessa's mom said. "I'm sure that Tessa appreciates it. And you are welcome to visit anytime."

Tessa walked back into her room. She listened as her mom let them out the door. She lay across the bed and waited. Knowing her mom, this was not over. She was right.

"Tessa Reese, I don't know what has gotten into you, but it isn't pretty."

"Mom, I just didn't . . ." Tessa started to say.

"Stop right there! Dini and Sefu left you a gift. I'm not sure why they are being so nice to someone who is treating them so rudely. I've got a good mind not to give it to you. But instead, here it is. And you can spend the rest of the evening thinking about what you just did."

Tessa felt her mom laying something on her bed. Then she was gone, mumbling to herself as she walked down the hall.

Tessa sat up and reached for whatever her mom had left on the bed. She felt badly about the way she had treated the twins, but she just wasn't in the mood for company. As she felt for the gift, her fingers found a flat box. She opened it and felt around to see what was inside.

She could hardly believe it. It was a Braille sports magazine and a note in Braille. Tessa's fingers trembled as she read the Braille note.

Dear Tessa,

We wanted you to know that we are so happy to be helping you with track. We borrowed a book about running with a person who is blind. Our grandmother got it for us from the Georgia Regional Library for the Blind and Physically Handicapped. She also wrote this note for us in Braille. Well, actually, for me. Sefu thinks you don't want us as friends. But I don't believe that. I hope you like the magazine.

Your friend,
Dini

Tessa felt sick. She did appreciate the magazine. And Dini had gone to a lot of trouble to get this note written. Plus, they'd even read up on how to be a guide runner. How would Tessa face them at school the next day? What would she say to them? And then there was Phyllis and Bailey to worry about. If they saw Tessa talking to the twins, they would wonder what was up. And if Tessa became friends with the twins, Phyllis and Bailey would probably never talk to her again. It was such a dilemma!

That night Tessa tossed and turned in bed. She finally fell asleep, hoping that this was all a bad dream. She wished that when she woke up the next morning, the magazine, the note, and her problems with her friends would be just part of the dream, and that everything would be back to normal.

8

Working
as Planned

Monday morning was a blur. Much to Tessa's dismay, Bailey and Phyllis were still ignoring her.

At lunchtime, when the girls were making their way to a table, Bailey and Phyllis stopped abruptly in front of Tessa. Her tray slammed into Bailey's back, sending the silverware clanking to the floor. Before she could pick it up, she heard a voice.

"Hello, Tessa. It's me, Kathy. Glad to see you again. I've been thinking about what you told me about your friends. You're a special person to say such nice things to help your friends. See you around, girlfriend."

"Oh my goodness," Bailey said. "Did you hear that? Kathy Walker is friends with Tessa."

"Wow!" said Phyllis. "You didn't tell us you knew Kathy that well. What did you tell her about us?"

Tessa couldn't believe it. This was much better than she'd imagined. Kathy actually spoke to her and called her "girlfriend." And now Phyllis and Bailey were speaking to her again. Tessa beamed as she said, "Well, I did tell her about my two good friends."

Bailey and Phyllis squealed with excitement.

Bailey said, "That's great. Hey, thanks, Tessa." She quickly looked at Phyllis and nodded. Then she turned back to Tessa. "Want to walk home with us today?"

"Sure." Tessa grinned. They were friends again, but for some reason she didn't feel as happy as she thought she would.

After school, Bailey and Phyllis waited for Tessa to get her things together in class. And for the first time in what seemed to be a very long time, they talked and laughed as they walked home together.

When Tessa got home, she sat on her swing in the backyard for a while. She wanted to read the letter she'd gotten back from Sabrina and sort out her feelings about having Phyllis and Bailey as friends again.

At dinner, Tessa barely spoke. While she washed the dishes, her mom asked, "What's the matter? You've hardly said a word all evening. Are you still having problems with Bailey and Phyllis? Is Bailey still upset about being bumped as a guide runner?"

"No, Mom. We're friends again," Tessa said.

"Then what is it?"

"I don't know," said Tessa. And she really couldn't put it into words.

Tessa wrote back to Sabrina that night. She thanked her for the letter and her suggestions for solving her problem. She told Sabrina about her plan and how it seemed to be working. She realized she had no reason to be sad. Bailey and Phyllis were her best friends again. Dini and Sefu were great guides and worked on different ways to help Tessa run faster. Each took turns running with Tessa on the track. Tessa was running faster than she had ever run and felt better and better about her running. She had asked the coach about allowing her to run against sighted kids in the big meet that was coming up. Coach Carolyn had said, "I'm thinking about it seriously. We'll see how you do this Friday at the team race."

And three weeks from now, when Kathy called Bailey and Phyllis up on stage to represent their school as good citizens, everything would be even better.

9

New Friends

The day before the team race, Dini and Sefu invited Tessa to eat dinner at their parents' restaurant. Tessa had never been to an Ethiopian restaurant before. It was different from any restaurant she'd ever eaten in, but the girls were very helpful and explained everything to Tessa as the dinner progressed. Everyone sat at handmade wicker hourglass-shaped tables called *mesabs*.

The twins' mother brought them a long-spouted copper pitcher and a copper bowl. She had a towel over her arm. Then she poured warm water over each of their fingers. The excess water dripped into the bowl. Then the twins' mother directed Tessa to wipe her hand on a towel. The table was covered with a tray that had a sourdough, pancake-like bread on top of it. The bread was called *injera* and was used in place of silverware. Dini showed Tessa how to eat

with her hands, tearing off a piece of the bread and picking up some food from the little piles on top of the bread.

Dinner included a spicy chicken stew called *Doro Watt* and a spicy lamb dish called *Yebeg Watt*. Tessa enjoyed all of it, except for the *Kitfo*, which was a raw ground-beef dish. After dinner, everyone washed their hands again at the table.

Tessa tried to remember the Ethiopian names of all the new things she had experienced. Dini and Sefu giggled at Tessa's mistakes, but Tessa didn't mind. Then the twins explained the meaning of their full names. Dini said, "Dinquinesh means 'she who is content or well-grounded.'"

Sefu said, "And Sefenech means, 'you are part of a large family.'"

Tessa said, "That's so interesting."

The twins' mother invited Tessa to their house after dinner. The girls showed Tessa some of their family's handwoven baskets that they had brought from Ethiopia and told her all about them. Tessa even got to take one of the small baskets home with her.

Tessa showed the basket to her mom

when she got home. Her mom liked it, and Justin thought it was cool.

Tessa was glad that Bailey and Phyllis were her friends again, but she couldn't deny that the twins had become her friends, too. Tessa was sorry that she hadn't tried to become friends with them sooner.

The night before the race, Tessa slept soundly, dreaming that she was running and that she never ran outside the lines of the track, not even once.

10

Team Race

It was the day of the team race. Sefu and Dini waited for Tessa at the entrance to the school track.

When Tessa approached, Sefu said, "Let's go win."

They had already decided that Sefu would be the guide for the 50-meter race and Dini would be the guide for the 100-meter race.

As they waited for Tessa's events, Tessa was so excited she could hardly stand it. She ran in place to burn off some of her nervous energy. Then Coach Carolyn announced it was time for runners in the 50-meter race to take their places. Tessa was positioned in the outside lane of the track. That meant that Sefu would be running at her left side and

Tessa wouldn't have to worry about a runner on her other side. She felt some of her nervousness melt away. She knelt in starting position, with Sefu at her side, holding the tether taut between them. Tessa's heart raced as she waited for the signal to run. When she heard the coach yell, "Go," Tessa ran as fast as she could, confident that Sefu would guide her. After what seemed like just a second, Tessa heard a cheer from the crowd

and she felt the tether go slack, which was her cue to stop. The race was over.

"Did I win?" she asked Sefu breathlessly.

"No, you didn't win, but you did OK," Sefu reassured her.

In the 100-meter race with Dini, Tessa ran as fast as she could. She didn't win that race either, but she didn't care. All she wanted was the satisfaction of knowing she ran a race with the sighted kids. And now she had that.

Coach Carolyn found Tessa and patted her on the back. "Tessa, it's me, and I have Kathy with me. We think you did a great job out there."

"Thank you, Coach Carolyn. Thanks, Kathy!" Tessa said. "I had fun."

"Good," Coach Carolyn said. "I want you to run in the big meet against Palmer Elementary next Saturday."

Tessa was delighted. "Wow! Thank you, Coach. Thank you so much. I couldn't have gotten better without your help—and the twins' help."

Kathy added, "They really are good guide runners. Hey, Dini, Sefu, come over here."

Tessa heard them coming over.

"Guess what? Coach says Tessa can race against Palmer Elementary next Saturday," Kathy said.

"That's wonderful," Dini said. "We'll help you practice every single day. Won't we, Sefu?"

"Sure. If she wants us to," Sefu said.

Tessa said, "You will?"

"Sure. We'll be there," Dini said.

Coach Carolyn said, "You girls are great. I hope you both are still planning to join the track team next year."

"Of course!" said both girls at the same time.

Dini said, "She's nice," as the coach walked away, discussing something with Kathy.

"Do you think I can win a race in the big meet?" Tessa asked. "I didn't win any of the races today."

"Sure you can," Sefu said. "We know you can do it. Our grandmother says people can do anything they set their minds to. She has a black belt in karate, and she's over sixty years old!"

During the next week, Tessa practiced

every day after school with Dini and Sefu's help. Tessa wrote to Sabrina to tell her how everything was falling into place. She felt so excited as Saturday—the day of the big meet—approached. Her mother, father, Justin, and her best friends, Bailey and Phyllis, would all be at the track meet. Tessa's dream was coming true.

11

Surprises

But Friday morning, the morning before the big meet, everything changed. It happened at the assembly when Kathy got up to make her announcement.

Kathy stood at the microphone and said, "We all know that it's time for the class president—that would be me—to select two students from each grade to represent our school as good citizens in the Good Citizen Awards Ceremony, which is a district-wide event. The people chosen will have the opportunity to attend a big dinner, will get an award, and know that they were chosen because they were kind, giving, and helpful to their fellow students."

A hush fell over the audience. Tessa could

have heard the tiniest pin drop on the floor.

Phyllis whispered excitedly, "She's going to choose us."

Bailey grabbed one of Tessa's hands and squeezed. She said, "Tessa, we know that it's because of you that we're being chosen. Thanks."

Tessa didn't dare breathe. She waited. If Bailey and Phyllis were chosen, Tessa would be so happy. That would mean the two would be her friends forever. Tessa was sure of it. She took in a deep breath.

Kathy was still talking on and on about what an honor it was to be named a Good Citizen. Then Kathy said, "One of the qualities we look for in choosing the Good Citizens is a willingness to work unselfishly as part of a team. This year, we're proud to have a perfect example of students working together for the good of all."

"Yeah," the kids shouted.

Kathy said, "Drum roll, please!"

The drummers in the school band beat their drumsticks hard and fast.

Tessa's heart pounded even faster than the drummer's rhythm as she waited to hear

Bailey and Phyllis' names called. Bailey squeezed Tessa's hand tightly.

"Are you ready?" Kathy screamed.

The kids were going wild now, singing "Yes, we're ready. Boom, boom. Yes, we're ready."

Tessa wasn't sure she could hear over all the noise.

Kathy shouted, "Our fourth-grade Good Citizens this year are . . ." Kathy paused and took a deep breath. Then she continued, "Sefenech and Dinquinesh Girma."

Tessa felt Bailey let go of her hand.

Bailey said loudly, "What?" But Kathy wasn't finished.

Before Tessa could say anything, the next announcement hit Tessa's ear like a thunderbolt.

"This year," Kathy shouted, "for the first time ever, we have a third Good Citizen for the fourth grade. This person is hard-working and tries to do her best for everyone. Her name is Tessa Reese."

Tessa's heart sank. The cheers of her classmates surrounded her, but she paid no attention to them. She could only think about how her plan had failed. Bailey and Phyllis didn't say a word to Tessa.

Tessa felt a hand on her shoulder and heard Coach Carolyn say, "Tessa, it's me. Give me your hand. I'll lead you up onto the stage. I bet you're surprised about this."

Tessa couldn't speak. She was most definitely surprised, but this would ruin everything. At least, that's what she thought as she moved toward the stage.

12

Tessa Takes a Stand

The trouble began at lunch shortly after the morning assembly. Tessa had almost forgotten that she'd invited Dini and Sefu to sit with her at lunch. She had figured that by then Bailey and Phyllis would have been named good citizens and everything would be fine. And then she'd call Bailey and Phyllis over and they'd all eat together to celebrate the upcoming defeat of the Palmer Timber Wolves by their school's track team at the big meet.

Now there was no chance that Bailey and Phyllis would want to be friends with Dini and Sefu. She didn't hear Phyllis and

Bailey's voices in the lunch line. But to her relief, she didn't hear Dini or Sefu, either.

But her relief didn't last very long. "Here we are," Dini said. "Isn't it great that we were all chosen as Good Citizens?"

Tessa heard a familiar, angry voice behind her. "Why don't you and your friends hurry up?" said Bailey as she stepped in line.

"Come on, Bailey, don't be mad because Kathy chose Dini and Sefu instead of you and Phyllis," Tessa said.

"She chose them because you told her to. You never told Kathy about Phyllis and me. You told her about your new buddies instead," Bailey shouted.

"That's not true," Tessa said. "I did tell her about you and Phyllis. But I guess she saw what good team members Dini and Sefu are."

"You're not my friend anymore. Or Phyllis' friend, either. In fact, no one wants to be friends with you *or* the twins," said Bailey.

Tessa had had enough. "Bailey, you're being really mean," she said, determined to stand up for herself and her new friends.

"Are you talking to me, Miss Traitor?" Bailey asked.

"Yes," Tessa said. "And I'm not a traitor. Kathy picked the twins because they deserved it. You're not being fair."

Bailey said, "Yes I am. Aren't I, Phyllis?"

Tessa moved her head in Phyllis' direction. She knew Phyllis was there because she could smell peppermints.

Bailey spoke again, but louder this time. "Phyllis, go ahead. Tell her I'm being fair."

Tessa didn't know why Phyllis wasn't answering. Was she really there?

Finally she heard a faint voice say, "Sometimes you're *not* fair—like right now."

It *was* Phyllis. Tessa was sure it was her voice.

"Bailey, Tessa's right. You're always trying to tell people what to do. And you get angry when things don't go your way and then you blame other people. *That's* not fair. Just like Tessa said," Phyllis said in a steadier voice.

Tessa couldn't believe it. Phyllis was finally standing up for herself, too.

"Now you've turned Phyllis against me," Bailey said angrily. "Well, I don't care. You and Phyllis can be friends with Dini and Sefu instead of being friends with me."

Then Tessa said, "They're already good friends of mine." The minute she said it, Tessa realized how good it felt to admit it. It was true. Dini and Sefu were her very good friends. Neither of them had ever threatened to take their friendship away. *That's* what being a good friend really means.

Tessa grabbed her tray and said, "I hope you change your mind. I don't see why we all can't be friends." Then Tessa said to Phyllis, "Would you like to eat with us?"

"OK," Phyllis answered. "I'm sorry I was mad at you."

"It's all right," Tessa said. "We all make mistakes. I'm just glad we could fix this one."

13

A Dream Come True

It was Saturday, the big day—the day of the track meet. When Tessa's mom called her to the phone, Tessa was afraid it might be Coach Carolyn saying she'd changed her mind about letting Tessa run. Tessa picked up the telephone. She was shocked to hear the voice on the other end.

"Hello. It's me . . . Bailey."

"Hello," Tessa said.

"I'm calling to wish you luck. You were right. I haven't been very nice to you lately," Bailey said in a tight, funny voice.

"Last night I was cleaning out my room and I found the friendship bracelet you gave me last year. You said we would be friends no matter what—'one for all and all for one.' I'm . . . sorry," Bailey stammered.

"It's OK. We've all been upset with each other lately. I think we'll always be friends. But I have to tell you—I still want to be friends with Dini and Sefu. They really are nice," Tessa said. She felt good about sticking up for the twins. "Are you coming to the meet today? Dini, Sefu, and Phyllis will be there. Then we can all be friends."

"No, I don't know if I want to be friends with them," Bailey said. And then, in almost a whisper, Bailey said, "And I don't know if they want to be friends with me."

"Well, OK, if that's how you feel," Tessa sighed, "but thanks for calling me anyway."

"You're welcome," Bailey said and quickly hung up.

Tessa told her mom about the phone call. She assured Tessa that Bailey would come around.

Once they arrived at the track meet, Tessa's mom, dad, Justin, and Phyllis stood on the sidelines near the team. Tessa was nervous. With her cane held in front of her,

Tessa paced back and forth like a caged cat.

Dini and Sefu met up with Tessa and led her to where some of the earlier races were being run. As the twins watched each event, Dini and Sefu took turns describing to Tessa what was happening. They made her feel like a part of everything.

At last it was Tessa's turn to run. Tessa heard the runners lining up for the 100-meter race. Shouts from the crowd let Tessa know that a large crowd of people surrounded the track. This made her even more nervous. Normally, there were only a few spectators around when Tessa ran.

"You're going to do fine," Dini said. "Right, Sefu?"

"Sure," Sefu said. "You've been running perfectly in practice. You'll be OK."

"What if they laugh at me?" Tessa asked.

"Laugh with them," was the last advice Sefu offered.

Sefu helped Tessa onto the track.

Sefu whispered, "Remember what my grandmother said—you can do anything you want to do."

Tessa nodded. She ran in place trying to

quiet her nerves. Fear gripped her stomach. What if she fell? What if she didn't hear the signal to run? It was very noisy. There was much more noise at the meet than at the track at school. Tessa couldn't quiet her nerves.

Coach Carolyn came up behind her and reassured her. "Don't worry. You'll do fine."

Sefu was faster than Dini, so she was chosen to run with Tessa for the 100-meter race. Two other girls were running from the other school's team, plus one other girl from her own team.

Tessa could hear some of her teammates saying, "Go get 'em, Tessa."

She could hear Sefu's breathing beside her as they knelt in position. Tessa held the tether tightly. If Tessa was going to back out, now was the time. Tessa squeezed her eyes and lifted her head up. I can do this. I can do this, she said over and over in her mind. Tessa tilted her head toward the sideline where the start would be called out.

Justin shouted, "Go, Sis."

"That's my girl over there." Tessa heard

her dad's voice as it boomed over the crowd.

Tessa was usually positioned either on the inside or outside lanes of the track. That way, the only person running beside her was her guide runner. But a mistake was made and Tessa was positioned in the third lane. That meant that Sefu was on Tessa's left side and another runner was on Tessa's right. Now Tessa had the additional fear that she might accidentally drift into the other runner's lane. She had to depend on Sefu to help her stay in her own lane.

Tessa squeezed the tether even tighter. She could feel the tension in it. That tension reminded Tessa that Sefu would help her stay in her lane.

Only seconds later, Tessa heard "Go!" and raced forward. She held the tether firmly in her fist. Loud cheers rang out on either side of her.

Tessa pumped her legs up and down. She leaned her body forward and ran. Tessa's arm brushed the runner on her right. Tessa realized suddenly that she was drifting into the other runner's lane.

Tessa felt Sefu tightening the tether just enough to pull her back into the center.

Tessa took deep breaths to fill her lungs with air. She heard the thunder of her heartbeat. Suddenly, she heard a loud roar from the crowd. She knew she must have come across the finish line. Tessa leaned over, panting. She walked a few steps to keep her

legs from cramping as she caught her breath.

Sefu grabbed Tessa, shouting, "You did it! You did it!"

For a second, Tessa felt confused as she heard the crowd exploding. Then Tessa felt herself surrounded by family and friends.

"It's me, Coach Carolyn. Tessa, you came in second!"

Tessa couldn't believe it!

Tessa heard her mom and dad screaming at the top of their lungs. She heard Dini and Sefu, and could make out Phyllis' voice. But Bailey's voice was missing.

Tessa wobbled as everyone hugged and patted her back, shoulders, arms, and even her head. She felt wonderful.

It seemed that she was surrounded for a long time. Finally, Tessa heard her dad say, "Okay. That's enough. Move back, give her some air."

Tessa felt the cool air opening around her.

"You were great," her dad said. He gave her the biggest hug ever.

"Dini, Sefu," Tessa called. "Thank you. Thank you so much for being my guide team. And thanks for being my friends."

Justin squeezed Tessa's hand. He said, "Good job, Sis."

Tessa felt her friends close around her. A hand touched her shoulder. It was then that Tessa recognized a familiar scent of strawberries. Bailey had come after all.